This
Ready Set Read
book belongs to:

_____

My Reading Tree!

I'm a
Super
reader!

For Kate and Anna
~ E.B.

For Louise,
from Greg!

LITTLE TIGER PRESS

An imprint of Magi Publications

1 The Coda Centre, 189 Munster Road,

London SW6 6AW

www.littletigerpress.com

First published in Great Britain 2005

by Little Tiger Press, London

This edition published 2011

Printed in China

LTP/1800/0260/0611

ISBN 978-1-84895-369-7

2 4 6 8 10 9 7 5 3 1

MEGGIE MOON

ELIZABETH BAGULEY

illustrated by
GREGOIRE MABIRE

LITTLE TIGER PRESS

I♡reading!

5

Digger and Tiger spent
all their time in the Yard.
Nothing grew there but
piles of dented things,
empty things, worn-out
things. No one else
dared come to the Yard.
It was *their* place.

Digger and Tiger were
rough-and-tumble boys,
spiky-haired, hole-at-the-knee
boys. They were not brothers,
but they went together like
a trash can and its lid.

One day a girl arrived.
She walked through the
high gate and clicked it
shut behind her. She stared
at the tangled rubble and
the king-of-the-castle boys.
The boys stared back.

"I'm Meggie Moon,"
said the girl. "Can I play
with you?"

"We don't play with
girls," snarled Tiger.

"Girls don't know
how to play," hissed
Digger.

"Oh, they don't?"
said Meggie, laughing.

Meggie left the boys standing in
the shadows and went to explore.
The Yard was a mess and the
boys were unfriendly, but Meggie
had ideas.

She picked up some of the
junk and began
to arrange it . . .

a tin can here and
a pipe there . . .

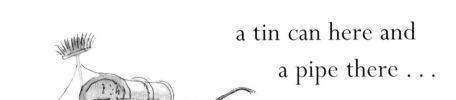

until . . .

"It's a racing car!" said Tiger.
"You can drive it if you want,"
offered Meggie.
"Not likely," said Digger.

But as soon as Meggie left,
the boys jumped into the car
and raced away until dark.

The next day Meggie
came to the Yard again.
Digger and Tiger
watched her picking
through the junk.

"Go on, then, build
something!" ordered
Tiger.

So Meggie made
a ship. When it was
finished, the boys
played pirates.

"Can I come
aboard?" she asked.

"I suppose you
could be our cook,"
said Tiger.

"I'd rather be your lookout," said Meggie.
She spat on her hands, shot up the
rigging, and shouted, "Enemy ship ahoy!"
Startled, the boys drew their swords.
"Aye-aye, shipmate!" they said.

By the third day the
car was mangled and
the ship wrecked.

"Let's kick cans,"
suggested Tiger.

"I'd rather throw
stones," said Digger.

"That's boring," said
Meggie. "Let's make
a den."

She found wall-things
and roof-things, and
the boys crammed and
jammed them into
a corner. They played
until dark, when the
bed calls came.

Every day
Meggie thought
of something different.
They crossed a snake pit,
shivered through a haunted
castle, lurched around
a roller-coaster . . .
   "She's not bad—for a
girl," Digger admitted
to Tiger, secretly.

Then, one day, Meggie announced,
"I'm going home tomorrow."
    The boys gazed at the Yard.
They remembered how, before Meggie
came, the rubble was just rubble.
    "But what will we play?"
wailed Digger.

"I've brought you a good-bye present.
You can play with that." Meggie
wheeled in a towering load and
toppled it in front of them.

"Space explorers at
the ready!" she
commanded, then
marched out through
the gate, clicking it
shut behind her.

"Aye-aye, Captain,"
Digger and Tiger saluted,
but Meggie had gone. The
sound of the closing gate
echoed through the Yard.

The boys stared sadly after Meggie. At last they inched toward her present-pile. The heap of rubble was just . . . a porthole here, a jet there . . .

The boys looked at each other.

They had ideas.

"Space explorers!" barked Digger.
"At the ready!" shouted Tiger.

By dusk, smooth things
and crumpled things,
shattered things and
battered things
spiraled high
above the
Yard fence.

With spacesuits on, the astronauts
climbed into the rocket.

"Blast off!" they chorused. With
a roar and a rumble, the rocket burst
into life, and Digger and Tiger
zoomed into space—away, away from
the Yard in the *Starship Meggie Moon*.

Picture Dictionary

Look at the words below and put the correct
picture sticker next to each word.

can

flag

flower

mouse

junk

sock

★ Have you got these right?
Then put a star on your reading tree!

26

Neat Nouns

noun is a person, place, or thing. Add the missing nouns
the sentences below with the word stickers.

rocket – gate – ship – astronauts – Yard – girl

) Digger and Tiger spent all their time in the _____ .

) One day a _____ arrived.

) So Meggie made a _____ .

) The sound of the closing _____ echoed through
the Yard.

) With spacesuits on, the _____ climbed into

the _____ .

Can you find these sentences in the story?

★ Did you get all the nouns right? Great!
Add another star to your reading tree.

Super Search

Look at the picture below. Put the word stickers next to the correct objects in the picture. We've done one for you.

lid

⭐ When you have put all the words in the right places, add a star to your reading tree!

28

Drawing

Let's get creative! Draw a picture in the frame for each word below.

castle	trash can	present

★ Did you draw all three pictures?
Add another star to your reading tree!

Lost Letters!

Oh, no! Some of the letters in the words from the story have disappeared. Write the missing letter in each word, using the letters from the box.

a – ~~e~~ – ~~i~~ – ~~o~~ – u

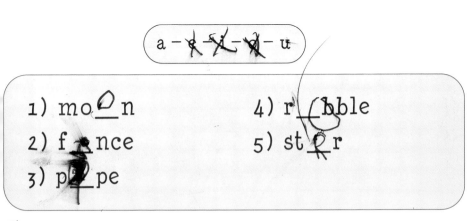

1) mo_o_n

2) f_e_nce

3) p_i_pe

4) r_u_bble

5) st_a_r

★ Could you spell the words right?
Don't forget to add another star to your reading tree!

Sentence Order

All stories are made up of **sentences**. Tick the sentence below that came **first** in the story.

☐ No one else dared come to the Yard.

☐ It was their place.

☐ Digger and Tiger spent all their time in the Yard.

Cool Questions

Some sentences are questions. You know when a sentence is a question because it has a **question mark** at the end of it

Put a **question mark** at the end of the sentences that are questions. Put a **period** at the end of the sentences that are not questions.

Can I play with you?

You can drive it if you want .

Let's make a den

But what will we play?

You can play with that.

★ Did you get the sentences and questions right?
Remember to add two more stars to your reading tree!